DRACULA

Written by Russell Punter

Based on the novel by Bram Stoker

Illustrated by Valentino Forlini

Series editor: Jane Chisholm

Consultant: Mike Collins

The World of Dracula
Europe 1897

SCOTLAND

North Sea

DENMARK

Whitby

IRELAND

WALES

ENGLAND

Amsterdam

NETHERLANDS

GERMANY

Hampstead Purfleet

London

BELGIUM

Exeter

Atlantic Ocean

FRANCE

SWITZERLAND

ITALY

PORTUGAL

SPAIN

May 3rd, 1897

Dear Mr. Harker,

Welcome to the Carpathians. I am anxiously expecting you.

Sleep well tonight. At three o'clock tomorrow the coach will start for Bukovina; a place on the coach is kept for you.

At the Borgo Pass my servant will await you and will bring you to me.

I trust that your journey from London has been a happy one, and that you will enjoy your stay in my beautiful land.

Your friend,
Count Dracula

BUT AT THAT MOMENT...

WOOOAH!

YOU'RE **EARLY** TONIGHT, DRIVER.

MY ENGLISH PASSENGER, **HERR JONATHAN HARKER,** WAS IN A **HURRY...**

NOT LONG AFTER...

TWELVE O'CLOCK!

TIME FOR **THE END OF THE WORLD**, IF THAT OLD LADY IS TO BE BELIEVED!

AT THAT MOMENT...

HOOOOWWWWLLL!

WHAT ON EARTH WAS **THAT**?

THE CARRIAGE TRAVELS ON...

...UP, THROUGH THE MOUNTAINS...

...HIGHER AND HIGHER...

...UNTIL AT LAST...

COUNT DRACULA?

I AM DRACULA. I BID YOU WELCOME, MR. HARKER.

COME IN! THERE IS A CHILL IN THE NIGHT AIR AND YOU MUST BE TIRED AND HUNGRY.

PLEASE, FOLLOW ME TO YOUR ROOMS.

WHAT A SINISTER PLACE!

YOUR ROOMS...

FOR SOME REASON, HE REMINDS ME OF THAT STRANGE DRIVER OF HIS. EVEN HIS VOICE SOUNDS THE SAME!

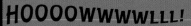

JONATHAN SLEEPS UNTIL THE EARLY AFTERNOON. WHEN HE RISES TO DRESS...

MY LITTLE **SHAVING MIRROR** WILL HAVE TO DO.

THAT'S **STRANGE**. THERE DOESN'T SEEM TO BE A **MIRROR** ANYWHERE.

AFTER ENJOYING THE COLD FOOD LEFT OUT FOR HIM...

AH, A **LIBRARY** OF SORTS...

I CAN **HARDLY** ROAM THE CASTLE UNTIL MY HOST HAS **RETURNED**. BUT WHAT'S THROUGH **HERE**, I WONDER?

THE COUNT HAS QUITE A COLLECTION, ALL RELATING TO **ENGLAND** I NOTICE...

SUDDENLY...

I'M GLAD YOU FOUND YOUR WAY IN **HERE**, MR. HARKER!

AS YOU SEE, I'M MOST KEEN TO **IMPROVE** MY **KNOWLEDGE** OF **YOUR COUNTRY**.

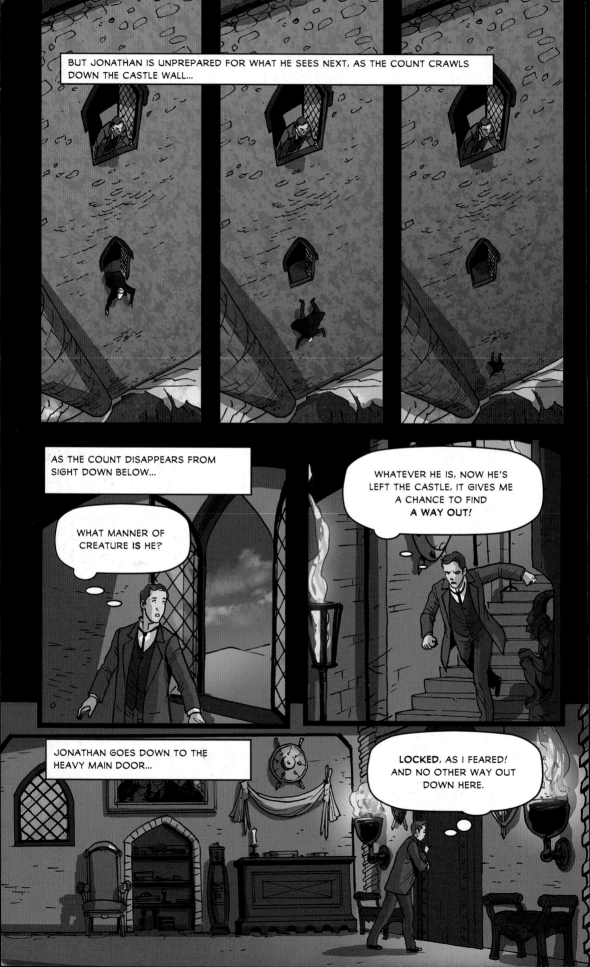

IT IS A **VILE** THING, AN **OUTRAGE** TO HOSPITALITY. BUT IT'S NOT SIGNED, SO IT CAN'T MATTER TO US.

AS IF THAT BLOW WEREN'T BAD ENOUGH, WHEN JONATHAN ENTERS HIS ROOMS...

ALONG WITH THE STATIONERY TOO! THIS MUST BE **DRACULA'S** DOING. IT'S A GOOD JOB I KEEP MY OWN NOTEBOOK AND PENCIL WITH ME!

ALL MY MONEY AND TRAVEL DOCUMENTS – **GONE!**

FOR A WHILE, JONATHAN BECOMES RESIGNED TO HIS FATE. NEARLY SIX WEEKS PASS. ONE AFTERNOON, HE SEES TWO WAGONS DRIVE INTO THE COURTYARD...

HEY, YOU DOWN THERE! HELP ME PLEASE!

A DELIVERY OF **BOXES**. ALL **EMPTY** BY THE WAY THEY'RE BEING HANDLED.

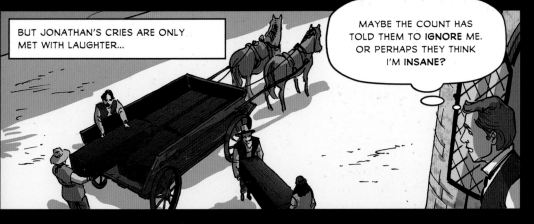

BUT JONATHAN'S CRIES ARE ONLY MET WITH LAUGHTER...

MAYBE THE COUNT HAS TOLD THEM TO **IGNORE** ME. OR PERHAPS THEY THINK I'M **INSANE?**

ANOTHER WEEK OF IMPRISONMENT DRAGS BY...

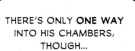

I NEVER SEE DRACULA DURING **DAYLIGHT.** MAYBE HE **SLEEPS** ALL DAY?

IF SO, I **MIGHT** BE ABLE TO **SEARCH** HIS ROOMS FOR A **KEY** OR SOME OTHER MEANS OF ESCAPE WHILE HE **SLEEPS.**

THERE'S ONLY **ONE WAY** INTO HIS CHAMBERS, THOUGH...

HERE GOES...

MUST FIND THAT KEY...

THEN...

OH NO!

IN DESPERATION, JONATHAN GRABS A NEARBY SHOVEL...

AS HE SWINGS THE MAKESHIFT WEAPON, THE COUNT RISES, HIS EYES BLAZING HORRIFICALLY...

JONATHAN'S GLANCING BLOW HAS LITTLE EFFECT...

SHUMP!

...SO HE FLEES IN TERROR...

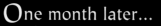

NEARLY TWO THOUSAND MILES FROM TRANSYLVANIA, IN THE SEASIDE TOWN OF WHITBY, ENGLAND, JONATHAN'S FIANCÉE MINA IS SPENDING THE SUMMER WITH HER FRIEND LUCY WESTENRA...

IS THERE ANY **NEWS** FROM **JONATHAN**, MINA?

MR. HAWKINS RECEIVED A LETTER, REGARDING JONATHAN'S **BUSINESS** WITH COUNT DRACULA...

BUT JONATHAN HASN'T WRITTEN TO YOU, **PERSONALLY?**

NO, WHICH IS **MOST** UNLIKE HIM.

OH, I'M MOST **TERRIBLY WORRIED**, LUCY!

I'M SURE HE'S WELL. IT'S SUCH A LONG WAY. HIS LETTERS MUST JUST HAVE BEEN LOST IN THE MAIL.
YES, YES. I'M SURE YOU'RE RIGHT...
...SO LET'S TALK OF HAPPIER THINGS, DEAR LUCY. YOUR THREE RECENT MARRIAGE PROPOSALS, FOR INSTANCE...
OH, MINA, I WAS GOING TO WAIT UNTIL AFTER I'D TOLD MAMA, BUT I MUST TELL YOU NOW. I'VE ACCEPTED ARTHUR!
CONGRATULATIONS! WERE MR. MORRIS AND DR. SEWARD TERRIBLY HEARTBROKEN?
THEY WERE BOTH MOST GALLANT. I'M PLEASED TO SAY IT HASN'T AFFECTED THEIR LONG FRIENDSHIP WITH ARTHUR.
SO YOU ARE TO BE MRS. HOLMWOOD.
OR LADY GODALMING, PERHAPS. SADLY ARTHUR'S FATHER, LORD GODALMING, IS UNWELL AND MAY NOT LIVE TO SEE US MARRIED.

AS MINA AND LUCY HEAD HOME, THE CLOUDS SUDDENLY DARKEN, AND THE TWO WOMEN COME ACROSS THE LOCAL COASTGUARD OFFICER...

GOOD EVENING, MR. TREGENNIS!

FOR US ON **LAND, MAYBE** LADIES. BUT I WOULDN'T WANT TO BE ON THAT SHIP **OUT THERE!**

IT'S AS IF THERE WAS **NO ONE** AT THE **WHEEL.** SHE **CHANGES COURSE** WITH EVERY **PUFF** OF THE **WIND!**

SHE'S A **RUSSIAN** VESSEL, BY THE LOOK OF HER. BUT SHE'S MOVING IN THE **ODDEST** WAY!

WITH THIS **STORM** COMING, WE'LL HEAR **MORE** ABOUT HER BEFORE THIS TIME TOMORROW!

GOOD NIGHT, MR. TREGENNIS.

GOOD NIGHT LADIES. **TAKE CARE!**

MEANWHILE, CAUGHT IN THE RAGING STORM, THE MYSTERIOUS RUSSIAN SHIP LURCHES TOWARDS THE CLIFFS...

...AND RUNS AGROUND ON THE SAND...

CRASH!

A SEARCH OF THE DEAD MAN'S POCKETS REVEALS A BOTTLE CONTAINING A SHEAF OF PAPERS...

IT LOOKS LIKE THE SHIP'S LOG...

WHEN THE RUSSIAN MANUSCRIPT IS TRANSLATED, IT TELLS A GRIM TALE OF THE *DEMETER*'S FINAL VOYAGE...

July 6th, Varna
Finished taking in cargo of fifty boxes of earth. Set sail at noon. East wind, fresh. Crew – five hands, two mates, cook and myself (captain).

July 13th, Cape Matapan
Crew seemed scared about something, but would not speak out.

July 16th
One of the crew, Petrofsky, missing. Could not account for it.

July 17th
One of the men, Olgaren, thought there was a strange man aboard ship. He saw a tall, thin man in a top hat go up on deck and then vanish. We searched the whole ship, but found no strangers.

July 24th, The Bay of Biscay
Another man lost last night – disappeared just like the first.

July 29th
Morning watch went on deck to find no one except steersman. We are now without second mate, and crew is in a panic.

July 30th, nearing England
Woken by mate telling me that man of watch and steersman are missing. Now only myself, mate and two hands left to work the ship.

August 1st
Two days of fog. No other ship sighted. We seem to be drifting towards some terrible doom.

August 2nd, midnight
A cry on deck. Rushed up to find man on watch gone. Lord, help us! Must be past Straits of Dover now. Only God can guide us in the fog, and He seems to have deserted us.

August 3rd, midnight
Went to relieve man at the wheel to find him gone. Shouted down to mate who came up, wild-eyed. Says he saw the stranger last night and stabbed at him, but the knife went through him as if through air.

He thinks 'it' must now be in one of the crates. Let him go below to search, while I remained at the helm.

Mate returned, convulsed with fear. He cried out to be saved, before throwing himself into the sea.

Surely he must be responsible for all the deaths? Only me left. God help me! How will I explain all this if I ever get to port?

August 4th
Still fog. In the dimness of the night I saw 'him'.

But I shall baffle this monster. I shall tie my hands to the wheel, along with something he cannot touch. I will have to pull the last knot tight using my mouth, but I know it can be done.

If we are wrecked, perhaps this bottle will be found and people will know that I have been true to my trust.

Heaven help me.

THE CAPTAIN'S TALE SOON APPEARS IN THE LOCAL NEWSPAPER, ALONG WITH A MORE RECENT TRAGEDY...

LOCAL MAN FOUND DEAD

Mr. Joshua Swales (76) was found dead on the bench outside the churchyard of St. Mary's Parish church in the early hours of this morning by local dog walkers. On examination by a physician, he was discovered to have a broken neck. Eyewitnesses at the scene say Mr. Swales had his head tipped right back and there was a look of fear and horror on his face that made them shudder. As yet, no evidence has been obtained regarding possible suspects, although a large dog was seen running from the churchyard shortly before the body was discovered.

POOR MR. SWALES!

AND IN OUR PEACEFUL SPOT BY THE CHURCH TOO!

LUCY SEEMS PARTICULARLY DISTURBED BY THE RECENT EVENTS. SHORTLY AFTERWARDS, MINA WAKES IN THE NIGHT TO FIND HER FRIEND'S BED EMPTY...

LUCY! SHE MUST BE SLEEPWALKING AGAIN!

I HAVE TO REACH HER BEFORE SHE HAS AN ACCIDENT...

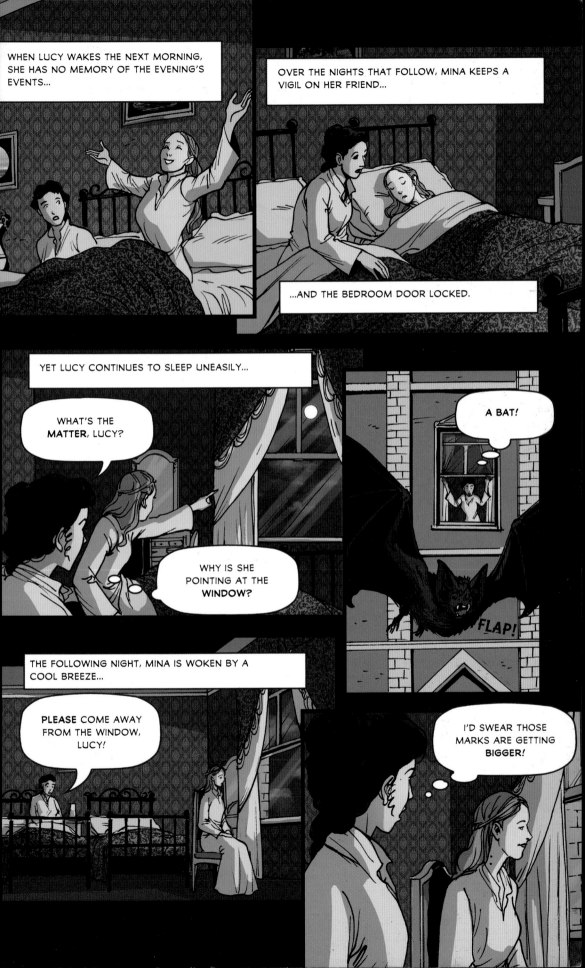

FOR THE NEXT FEW DAYS AND NIGHTS, JACK REMAINS AT LUCY'S BEDSIDE...

YOU'RE LOOKING **SO** MUCH BETTER, LUCY.

I **FEEL** IT. NOW YOU MUST REST IN YOUR ROOM TONIGHT. I'LL **CALL OUT** IF I NEED ANYTHING.

BUT WHEN THE TWO DOCTORS VISIT LUCY'S ROOM THE NEXT MORNING...

OH NO, SHE'S AS **WHITE** AS A **SHEET!**

NOW IT IS JACK'S TURN TO GIVE BLOOD...

AS LUCY RECOVERS...

WE MUST TAKE **PRECAUTIONS...**

FROM NOW ON, MISS LUCY MUST WEAR THIS GARLAND OF **GARLIC FLOWERS** AROUND HER NECK WHEN SHE SLEEPS.

I'M NEEDED **URGENTLY** BACK AT THE HOSPITAL. CAN YOU STAY WITH LUCY UNTIL I RETURN?

OF COURSE. I WILL SEND YOU A **TELEGRAM** IF I NEED YOU. NOW **ATTEND TO YOUR OTHER PATIENTS,** GOOD DOCTOR!

OBLIVIOUS OF THIS TRAGEDY, MINA AND JONATHAN, NOW NEWLY MARRIED, TRAVEL BACK TO ENGLAND...

I CAN'T WAIT TO GET HOME!

AT LAST THEY ARRIVE IN LONDON, FROM WHERE THEY PLAN TO CATCH A TRAIN TO EXETER...

...BUT ON THEIR WAY ACROSS THE CROWDED CAPITAL, JONATHAN SEES SOMETHING THAT CHILLS HIM TO THE BONE...

DRACULA!

UNAWARE HE IS BEING WATCHED, THE SINISTER FIGURE'S ATTENTION IS SET ON A BEAUTIFUL YOUNG WOMAN...

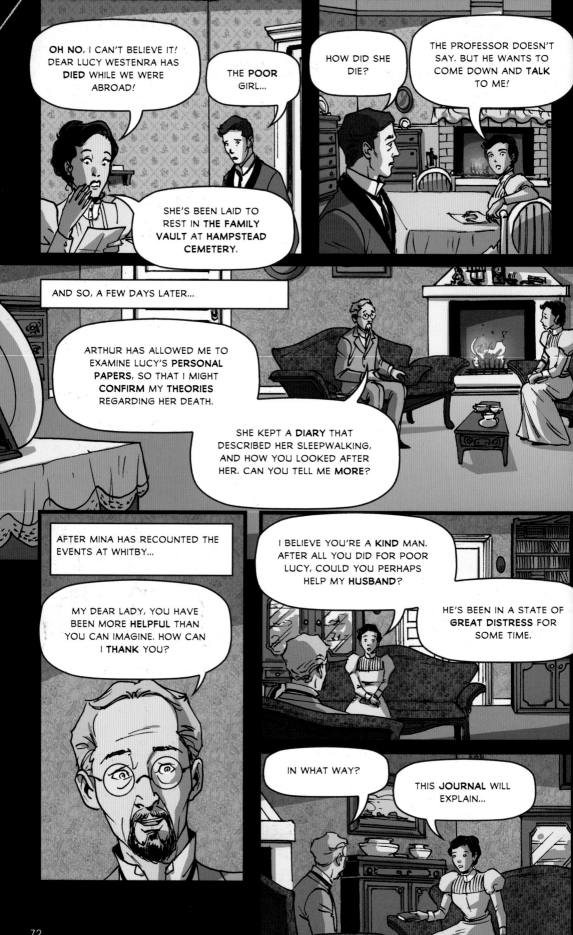

BUT AS THE DOCTOR SETTLES DOWN FOR HIS RETURN JOURNEY TO LONDON, A NEWSPAPER ARTICLE CATCHES HIS EYE...

THE HAMPSTEAD HORROR

In the past few days, several cases have been reported of young children going missing on the Heath in the early evening and not returning until morning. In each case, the children claim to have been with a 'beautiful lady'. All the children suffered wounds to the neck such as may have been made by a rat or small dog. When the latest victim was discovered, he was so weak that he was taken to hospital.

OH NO! SO SOON, SO SOON!

ON ARRIVAL IN LONDON, VAN HELSING RUSHES TO JACK'S HOSPITAL TO SHOW HIM THE ARTICLE...

I SUPPOSE THESE CHILDREN MUST HAVE **ATTACKED** BY THE **SAME THING** THAT BIT POOR LUCY...

IN A WAY, I WISH THAT **WERE** THE CASE!

WHAT DO YOU MEAN?

HAMPSTEAD IS WHERE **LUCY** IS BURIED. I BELIEVE SHE IS THE **'BEAUTIFUL LADY'** WHO **ATTACKED** THESE POOR CHILDREN!

BUT LUCY'S **DEAD!**

THE LUCY **YOU** KNEW, PERHAPS. BUT WHEN THE **VAMPIRE BAT** HAD DONE ITS WORK, IT LEFT AN **UNDEAD CREATURE** IN HER PLACE!

THE PROFESSOR VISITS ARTHUR TO EXPLAIN HIS THEORY AND THAT NIGHT, THE THREE MEN VISIT HAMPSTEAD CHURCHYARD...

TAKING A TURNSCREW FROM HIS BAG, THE PROFESSOR SETS TO WORK ON THE COFFIN LID...

SLIDE!

IT'S EMPTY!

THIS ONLY PROVES THAT HER **BODY**'S GONE, NOT THAT SHE'S STILL ALIVE.

QUITE SO. LET US SEEK THE **REAL PROOF** WE NEED...

THE TRIO CONCEAL THEMSELVES OUTSIDE THE VAULT AND WAIT...

TWO DAYS LATER, JACK IS JOINED BY HIS NEW HOUSE GUESTS. AFTER EVERYONE HAS SHARED THEIR EXPERIENCES...

SO LET US **CONSIDER** THE **ENEMY** WE FACE...

...THERE ARE SUCH BEINGS AS VAMPIRES. WHAT WE HAVE ALL **SEEN** PROVES THAT...

...I'VE STUDIED THE **LEGENDS** OF THESE CREATURES. THEY WERE ONCE **ORDINARY** MEN AND WOMEN. BUT WHEN **KILLED** BY THE BITE OF A **VAMPIRE**, THEY RETURNED TO LIFE AS UNDEAD VAMPIRES **THEMSELVES**.

IN ORDER TO **SURVIVE** THEY MUST DRINK THE **BLOOD** OF **HUMANS** TO REJUVENATE THEMSELVES, AND SO IT GOES ON...

THIS COUNT DRACULA MAY BE **CENTURIES** OLD. LIKE ALL HIS KIND HE WILL BE AS STRONG AS **TWENTY** MEN AND HAVE THE **DEAD** AT HIS **COMMAND**...

...NOT ONLY THE DEAD, BUT THE **ELEMENTS** TOO – **FOG, THUNDER, RAIN** ARE HIS TO CONTROL, AS WELL AS THE **BEASTS** OF THE ANIMAL KINGDOM. HE CAN USE HIS POWERS TO **SEE** THROUGH **THEIR** EYES.

HIS **INHUMAN POWERS** ENABLE HIM TO **CHANGE** HIS **SIZE**, TURN INTO **OTHER CREATURES** AND EVEN **VANISH** INTO THIN AIR...

WE KNOW HE HAS BROUGHT THE **EARTH** OF HIS HOMELAND TO THIS COUNTRY. ONLY ON SUCH SOIL, RICH WITH THE REMAINS OF HIS ANCESTORS, CAN A VAMPIRE **SLEEP**.

TO BRING SO **MUCH** EARTH MUST MEAN HE PLANS TO SET UP HOMES **ALL OVER** THIS LAND. **NOWHERE** WILL BE SAFE!

POOR LUCY WAS THE FIRST OF **HUNDREDS**, POSSIBLY **THOUSANDS**, OF VICTIMS... UNLESS THIS FIEND IS **STOPPED!**

BACK AT THEIR HOTEL, THE FRIENDS MAKE PLANS...

YES, WE HAD A **BOX**. IT WAS COLLECTED BY THE **SLOVAKS** WHO TRADE ALONG THE RIVER.

THE MOST LIKELY ROUTE FOR THEM TO TAKE FROM HERE WOULD BE UP THE **SERETH RIVER**, TO WHERE IT MEETS THE **BISTRITZA**. THAT RUNS UP AROUND THE **BORGO PASS**, NEAR **DRACULA'S CASTLE**.

Borgo Pass •
Bistritza River
Sereth River
Transylvania
Galatz •
ROMANIA
BULGARIA   Varna •

ARMED WITH WEAPONS TO DESTROY THE COUNT, THE SIX FRIENDS SET OFF. ARTHUR AND JONATHAN RENT A STEAM LAUNCH AND SET OFF UP THE SERETH RIVER...

...QUINCEY AND JACK FOLLOW ALONGSIDE THEM ON LAND...

...AND THE PROFESSOR AND MINA HEAD DIRECTLY TO DRACULA'S CASTLE...

AS THEY TRAVEL THROUGH EVER COLDER CONDITIONS, UP TO THE CARPATHIAN MOUNTAINS, THE PROFESSOR BECOMES MORE CONCERNED ABOUT MINA...

THE POOR GIRL REFUSES TO **EAT** AND NOW SHE **SLEEPS** MOST OF THE DAY!

I FEAR SHE IS CLOSE TO BECOMING A **VAMPIRE!**

AT LAST THEY REACH THE BORGO PASS. NOT LONG AFTER, CASTLE DRACULA COMES INTO VIEW...

IT WILL BE **SAFER** TO CAMP OUT **HERE** TONIGHT.

USING HIS KNOWLEDGE OF VAMPIRE LEGENDS, THE PROFESSOR DRAWS A CIRCLE IN THE GROUND AROUND THEM...

...AND SCATTERS CRUSHED HOLY WAFERS ALONG ITS EDGE...

NOW WE ARE **PROTECTED!**

AS NIGHT FALLS, THREE SHAPES SEEM TO FORM OUT OF THE DARKNESS...

THE PROFESSOR FINDS THE CASTLE DESERTED. USING A MAP PROVIDED BY JONATHAN AS A GUIDE, HE MAKES HIS WAY TO THE RUINED CHAPEL...

...WHERE HE KILLS THE THREE FEMALE VAMPIRES...

A FURTHER SEARCH LEADS HIM TO ONE MORE TOMB...

SO HE IS NOT YET **COME**. I'LL MAKE SURE HE CAN **NEVER** REST HERE AGAIN!

DRACULA

DRACULA

The Story of Dracula

Legends of demons that eat flesh and drink blood have existed for thousands of years. But the familiar vampires of modern stories have their origins in 17th and 18th century Eastern Europe.

In 1672, in what is now Croatia, a peasant named Jure Grando was said to have returned from the dead to drink the blood of the local villagers. When an attempt to kill him by driving a hawthorn stick through his heart failed, he was beheaded.

Jure Grando

Later, during what came to be known as the '18th Century Vampire Controversy', there were outbreaks of 'vampire' sightings across Eastern Europe, particularly in what is now Germany, as well as Serbia. The Serbian incidents included the case of Peter Blagojevich who supposedly returned from the dead to ask his son for food. When he refused, Blagojevich killed him before going on to attack some of the local villagers.

From the 18th century onwards, vampires found their way into popular fiction via poems and stories. One of the most popular early short stories was *The Vampyre* (1819) by John Polidori, an English writer and physician which featured the vampire Lord Ruthaven. In 1847 a character named Varney the Vampire appeared in Britain in a series of so-called 'penny dreadful' pamphlets.

The most famous vampire of all, however, was created by Bram Stoker in the late 19th century.

Varney the Vampire

Stoker was born in 1847 in Dublin, Ireland, and spent the first seven years of his life confined to bed due to illness. This long period of isolation gave him time to think up ideas for stories that he would later put to good use in his writing career.

After making a full recovery, he went on to study at university in Dublin. It was while he was there that he began a lifelong interest in stage plays, and later became a critic.

Henry Irving

After graduating from university, Stoker began writing short stories, the first of which was published in 1872. In 1876 he wrote a review of a play starring Henry Irving, one of the most famous actors of the time. Irving was so impressed that he and Stoker became lifelong friends.

After moving to London, Stoker was made the manager at Irving's Lyceum Theatre and began writing novels in his spare time.

The inspiration for the setting of his most famous work, *Dracula*, may have come from his meeting with a Hungarian writer Ármin Vámbéry, as Stoker himself never visited Eastern Europe. He did, however, spend many years researching European folklore and vampires, and also enjoyed trips to the English town of Whitby, where part of the novel is set.

As for the origins of the character of Dracula himself, Stoker claimed to have once had a nightmare featuring a vampire king rising from the dead. The dramatic mannerisms of the Count were said to be based on Irving, whom Stoker hoped would one day play the role on stage, although he never did.

The name Dracula derives from the Romanian word 'dracul' meaning either 'the dragon' or 'the devil'.

Up until a few weeks before publication, the title for the novel was *The Un-Dead*. When it was first published in 1897, the re-titled *Dracula* was not an immediate success, although it received excellent reviews.

It wasn't until some time after Stoker's death, in April 1912, that the novel became widely popular, due in part to the success of a German film version called *Nosferatu* that was released in 1922. Stoker's widow Florence had sued the film company for breach of copyright and all prints of the film were ordered to be destroyed. However some copies survived and were shown in cinemas to appreciative audiences.

Florence later agreed to license the story and it was adapted for the stage. A 1927 version featured the actor Bela Lugosi in the title role, which he would go on to repeat in the hugely successful Universal Studios film version of 1931. The character of Dracula was so popular, he continued to appear in many horror films of the 1930s and 40s.

In 1958, Hammer Film Productions released a version of the story featuring Christopher Lee as Dracula and Peter Cushing as Van Helsing. Over the following fifteen years, both actors reprised these roles many times.

On television, Louis Jourdan starred in a BBC adaptation in 1977. More recent film versions include *Dracula* (1979) and *Bram Stoker's Dracula* (1992).

The Count's plan for immortality may have failed, but in the real world, Stoker's creation will surely never die.

Count Dracula

Russell Punter was born in Bedfordshire, England. From an early age he enjoyed writing and illustrating his own stories. He trained as a graphic designer at art college in West Sussex before entering publishing in 1987. He has written over fifty books for children, ranging from original rhyming stories to adaptations of classic novels.

Valentino Forlini was born in Cremona, Italy, in 1970. He has been a comic book artist since 1996 and has worked for major publishers in Italy such as Star Comics on *Samuel Sand*, *Lazarus Ledd* and *Goccianera*, Eura on *John Doe* and Sergio Bonelli Editore on *Nathan Never* and *Le Storie*. Over the years, he has worked for the Walt Disney Company on various projects including *Chicken Little*, *The Wild*, *Lilo and Stich*, *Meet the Robinsons*, *Pirates of the Caribbean*, *Cars*, *Toy Story* and *Power Rangers*. Valentino is also a storyboard artist and has worked on several TV cartoon series including *Team Galaxy*, *MBC*, *Famous Five*, *Spiez*, *Gormiti* and *Stefi's World*.

Mike Collins has been creating comics for over 25 years. Starting on *Spider-Man* and *Transformers* for Marvel UK, he has also worked for DC, 2000AD and a host of other publishers. In that time he's written or drawn almost all the major characters for each company – *Wonder Woman*, *Batman*, *Superman*, *Flash*, *Teen Titans*, *X-Men*, *Captain Britain*, *Judge Dredd*, *Sláine*, *Rogue Trooper*, *Darkstars*, *Peter Cannon: Thunderbolt* and more. He currently draws a series of noir crime fiction graphic novels, *Varg Veum*. He also provides storyboards for TV and movies, including *Doctor Who*, *Sherlock*, *Warhammer 40K*, *Igam Ogam*, *Claude*, *Hana's Helpline* and *Horrid Henry*.

Cover design: Matt Preston

First published in 2017 by Usborne Publishing Ltd., Usborne House, 83-85 Saffron Hill, London EC1N 8RT, England. www.usborne.com
Copyright © 2017 Usborne Publishing Ltd.